Magic Moon Dreams

Written by Ellie Crowe
Illustrated by Kristi Petosa-Sigel

ISLAND HERITAGE

Published and distributed by

 ISLAND HERITAGE
P U B L I S H I N G

94-411 KŌʻAKI STREET, WAIPAHU, HAWAIʻI 96797
ORDERS: (800) 468-2800 • INFORMATION: (808) 564-8800
FAX: (808) 564-8877 • **islandheritage.com**

ISBN# : 0-89610-767-1

First Edition, Second Printing - 2005

To Sydney Elisabeth
with Love

A magic moon's rising,
Where shall we sleep?
Wherever we dare,
Anywhere!

3

We could sleep in the garden with tree frogs and geckoes,
With dragonflies, moon moths, mongooses, and mice.
We'll snuggle with them in some soft, starlit places,
That would be so nice!

4

We'd be snug as a bug with a furred caterpillar,
Then leave our cocoon with a bright butterfly.
We'd swing in a web with happy-faced spiders,
And watch stars go by.

Perhaps we'll dream with chameleons under the moon,
Or nap in a honeycreeper's nifty nest,
Curled up in a tree snail's striped red and white shell,
That's where we could rest.

If there should be a wild night of lightning and thunder,
When wind shakes the trees and rain falls from the sky,
Where would the animals sleep then, we wonder?
How could we keep dry?

We could nap in dark forests in a warm nene nest,
Or hang upside-down with small bats in a cave.
Would we be scared in such shivery places?
Oh no—we're too brave!

We could nestle in mounds with wobble-footed gooneys,
Or plop with fat bufos where mud's warm and runny,
Stilts sleep standing up, but who'd want to do that?
That's just too funny.

15

We could share sandy moon dreams on a
   beach with monk seals,
Or float fast asleep on a green turtle's shell.
Sand crabs dig deep, dark holes and sort of
   peek out,
We'd try that as well.

We could snap ourselves snugly in an
   oyster's pearl shell,
Or soak with starfish in a pool by the sea.
An octopus garden so shady and quiet,
Is where we could be.

A magic moon's rising,
Where shall we sleep?
This soft pillow nest,
Would be best!

20

We'll close our sleepy, dreamy eyes,
Goodnight, magic Hawai'i moon.

21

THE END